THE IPM DIARIES

CONFESSION OF A FUTURE LEADER – VOLUME 02

PRIYASHA BANERJEE

Dedicated to the incredible animals of CARE, whose unwavering spirit and resilience continue to inspire. May they find love, comfort, and a forever home

Contents

Preface

The pages of The IPM Diaries: Volume Two delve deeper into the vibrant tapestry of my IPM journey. Building upon the foundations laid in the first volume, this sequel invites you to experience the exhilarating highs and humbling lows of my second semester.

From the adrenaline-fueled excitement of SPEED, the cultural extravaganza of ATHARVA, to the creative energy of WAVES, these events have shaped not just my academic experience but also my sense of belonging. The camaraderie forged during these shared experiences has been invaluable, strengthening the bonds between my peers and creating lasting memories.

Beyond the classroom, I embarked on a transformative internship at Charlie's Animal Rescue Centre (CARE). This experience opened my eyes to the world of animal welfare and inspired me to make a positive impact.

This volume is a testament to the power of connection and the transformative nature of the IPM program. It's a journey of self-discovery, academic exploration, and personal growth. I hope it serves as a guide for future IPM aspirants, offering insights into the challenges and rewards of this demanding yet fulfilling program.

Acknowledgements

I would like to express my sincere gratitude to CARE for providing me with the invaluable opportunity to intern with them for six weeks. This experience has shaped my understanding of animal welfare and inspired me to make a positive impact.

I am eternally grateful to my parents for their unwavering love, support, and encouragement. My rabbits have been a constant source of joy and companionship, and I am blessed to have them in my life. My older sister has been my confidante and a pillar of strength, always there to offer guidance and support. To my dear grandmother, whose love knows no bounds, I owe a debt of gratitude.

I would also like to thank Kyra Jacob, my fellow intern, for capturing the beautiful cover photo featuring Captain and Veer.

Finally, I would like to thank my fellow batchmates for making my second semester at IPM an unforgettable experience. Their camaraderie, support, and shared experiences have enriched my academic journey.

CHAPTER ONE

A Semester Ends and Another Journey of Chaos Begins

07th January 2024

One semester just ended with so much learning, fun, drama, and getting used to doing everything by myself. Gave a good number of presentations, exams, and quizzes. I made many friends (really a lot, like too many necessary and unnecessary ones as well). It was a semester full of a lot of things. During the semester break, my family and I went on a vacation in Thailand, and not just the fun prospect but also culturally, I learned a lot of things that will help me academically and professionally one day. I got my social internship confirmed in Bangalore only. It's known as Charlie's Animal Rescue centrE (CARE). It is located in Yelanka, a beautiful and well-maintained non-profit organization. I met their manager, Mr Keerthan, and discussed my social internship with them. He agreed to it and suggested that I come up with a project for myself, and if it's feasible, they will go along with it; if not, they will give me a project. They also verified my internship by sending me an email. I enjoyed the remaining few days of my holiday with family, and as something new for the new year, I got my hair-coloured red highlights. The packing back to the hostel took a while as my clothes were everywhere. Well, starting tomorrow, my classes will begin. I would like to know what this semester has for me. I hope the enjoyment and learning are double that of the previous semester.

08th January 2024

It's the first day of a new semester, but it was way too chaotic for me personally. My train was 1 hour and 15 minutes late. It reached Udupi Railway station around 5:30 AM. Luckily, I met my batchmate Kuhu on board the same train. Upon arrival, Kuhu and I decided to take a taxi back to the hostel because the auto line was way too long. We had humungous luggage that could pass off as a mini human. As we even split the bill, the pricing was fine. Now, from here, the bigger problem begins. I realized I had forgotten my keys to my room at my house. Luckily, I had the spare key in my wallet. Now, I am at ease. I informed my parents that I had reached my room safely, and I cleaned my room a little bit. Then, I planned to rest for a while before showering. As I was about to unpack my suitcase, I realized I had also forgotten my cupboard keys. Now, I am not feeling that great, as it is too much nonsense for me to put up with. Internally, I am cursing myself for having goldfish memory, like, wow, Priyasha, you had one job and messed up big time. I repeat, Big Time! Luckily, I store clothes in my bed's drawers as well; otherwise, I would need more than the amount of clothes I have in my suitcase to last a week. Thankfully, my father's colleague visits his family every weekend in Udupi, and my father would be sending my keys with him. Devasted? Nope, that's not even the right word at this point; it's frustration, anger, annoyance, and rage; with all this, I go to bed until the sun actually rises cause all this nonsense happened when the sun wasn't even up, like seriously y'all this was a terrible morning to being my new semester with. After waking up and getting ready for class, I only have breakfast in my room. My mother had prepared pasta, which was something good and delicious, trying to save the remaining day.

My friends loved my new hair look, and I met Sneha, who also coloured her hair; we had almost the same colour and looked amazing, no kidding. First, we completed our registration for the second semester, but we had way too much free time; our classes weren't until the afternoon. We went to the library, collected our psychology textbook, and then spent the rest of our time in the Student Centre; we even had our lunch there and finally went back to K. K. Pai block for our class. The first class was Scientific Thinking, which was going to be taught to us by Prof Bhawana and Prof Manoj. They first explained the course outline, which had an interesting component: class participation. It was 30% of our evaluative component. We were briefly introduced to the first chapter, "What is Science and its Origin?" Then, we did a fun group activity and completed the first session. The next session was Foundations of Psychology, which was going to be taught to us by Professor Vidya and Professor Manoj. Prof Manoj is taking two courses for us this semester; he is also our co-chair of IPM and my FAS mentor. I will be seeing him a lot more than I expected. They also explained the course outline and even distributed our final project for this semester. Our team got "False Memory," and our mentor in this project is, once again, Professor Manoj only. At this point, he has just adopted us. Then Prof Vidya introduced us to psychology, and I enjoyed this session a lot as I have a keen interest in psychology, and I am finally getting a chance to learn it. Once we were back, we were all very tired, and I was working on Volume One, the previous book, and its editing.

09th January' 2024

Today, we only have two sessions. The first one is Business Mathematics, which is being taught to us by Professor Ritu Gupta. She also taught us last semester. It wasn't a new subject, but Ma'am changed her way of teaching and even the book. She taught us in a way that was much easier to understand, and she started with Matrix and its operations. I remembered some of it from my previous grades, which made the class a little better. The next session was Financial Accounting, which will be handled by Professor Nandan Prabhu this semester. Coincidentally, he was Professor Krishna Prasad's professor as well during undergrad. He is also a phenomenal professor. He then started from the basics to give us a recap of what we learned previously. He gave us a basic idea of Inventory and continued to teach us about it. After this, we were back at the hostel. Today was the opening for SPEED, but there was one issue: my jersey was inside my cupboard, and Manasvi tried breaking my cupboard open for 30 minutes straight, but nothing fruitful came out of it. We decided that I could camouflage with the crowd by wearing a shirt that is black and white. I succeeded in that. We got our class photo clicked, and then they inaugurated the ceremony with speeches and more. For the first time, we met our new director in this ceremony. Well, we did not speak or anything with him, but we saw him for the first time. He is Rajeeb Kumra, who was the previous Deam of IIM-Lucknow. Anyway, we had a Table Tennis match today; our team qualified all the way to the quarter-finals, which are tomorrow. Anyways it was damn cool and one hella energetic game to watch. Our class's players played exceptionally well, making this a fun game to watch. However, we forgot our umbrellas and got entirely drenched on the way. But anyway, today was super fun and tiring.

0th January'2024

Today, we have only one session, it is Business Mathematics, and it is in the second slot. I peacefully got ready and left for class. Ma'am continued with Matrices and Their operations; she explained the types of matrices and how to perform operations like addition, subtraction, scalar multiplication, and matrices multiplication. Once we were back, I got Mithra's jersey to wear; shc had different plans so that she wouldn't be attending today's quarter-finals. We played against Phoenix, and they were super good. We won women's singles and doubles but lost men's singles, doubles, and mixed. We did not qualify for the semi-finals, but it was a match worth watching. There were a few issues; one friend of mine was hurt, but nothing major happened to him. He is fine. But it was one hell of a chaotic day.

11th January' 2024

Today, we also have the exact timetable as yesterday. It was Business Mathematics, and today, we solved problems and got a better grasp of Matrices and their Operations. Well, we were informed by our class representatives and IPM Club representatives that regarding yesterday's disputes during the game, our Student Council wasn't very pleased. They wanted our behaviour to be better, and our representatives also took our opinions and pitched them regarding the same matter. Well, we all make mistakes, but admitting and learning from them and not repeating them is what they want us to do as well. Let's not dwell deeper on this, as I believe our representatives and SEC will do their best to solve this. Once we were back, I realized I had left a few more things at home that also needed to be sent over. My parents, at this point, were done with my goldfish memory and were disappointed in me. Well, I messed up big time. I once again started working on volume one of IPM Diaries. And then I had my dinner and bid the night good night.

CHAPTER TWO

Academia with SPEED; Unique new Rhythm

12th January' 2024

We initially had two sessions, but our first session was cancelled; during this time, I went to Kasturba to get a check-up on my skin issue. I finished up all that around 10 AM and was back in the hostel. Then we left for campus; our only session today was Financial Accounting, where sir taught us specific identification, FIFO, LIFO, and weighted average methods used in Inventory measuring and finding Cost of Goods Sold (COGS). We also solved a problem on this to get a better grip on this topic. After this class, we saw our TAPMI hoodies; they come in two colours: cream and navy blue. There are two versions: one is a hoodie, and the other is a zipper version. After that, we came to our hostel. I finally finished my part of Volume One, and now only Dad had to complete the final editing. I took a nap, and once I was up, I started watching a new series and then went for the so-called 'Monthly Special Dinner,' which wasn't as great as our exception. After that, we walked for a while, chatted briefly, and then returned to our rooms. It was one long , tiring day.

13th January' 2024

On the first Saturday of the second semester, we had only two classes today. First was business mathematics, where Ma'am taught us elementary row operations on matrices and helped us solve problems with them. I hated this part of matrices in my 12th; it always flips your brain, and the same thing happens again. The last session was Foundations of Psychology where ma'am taught us Schools of Psychology and asked us to search more on any one of the school of thoughts and we will discuss that next class. She told us her marathon stories as well, which was very inspiring to listen to. Then, we saw our final papers of the previous semester. I passed in all subjects, leaving Economics. But that's okay. I can improve this semester by writing the make-up exam. My parents also suggested the same and told me not to worry too much. Finally, my keys were here; yes, this isn't a drill. It is actually here. I first cleaned the cupboard and then rearranged all my clothes. Then I gave my laundry to wash. I also cleaned and stacked my study table as well. Then, as the dinner in the canteen was pathetic, I came right back up and decided to have pasta in my room, which was very good. After this, I watched a series that I had recently started and went to bed afterward.

14th January 2024

Today is our class boys' cricket match for SPEED against Falcons. It is in the morning, around 11 AM, at the endpoint. For the first time, not even in the first semester, did I ever wake up on a Sunday morning. I even had the first breakfast on Sunday at Manipal. Next, after I got ready,

Diva and I left for End Point. It was one long and tiring walk and took half of our energy out. We tossed and won the toss. Our boys decided to bat first; this match is 20 overs each. We played very well despite less practice and set a target of 147. We only lost two wickets, and Saptarshi, the opening batsman, was there till the last over. He played amazingly, and so did our entire team. In the end, we did lose, but it was a great match. Once we were back at the hostel, lunch time had passed long ago. It was already 4 in the afternoon. Sneha, Harshitaa, and I decided to have lunch at Butterfly Cafe. Well, Harshitaa, being the God of clumsiness and trying to save a big jug of water, dropped ice and lime entirely on Sneha and me instead. One thing off my bucket list is to take a piece of clothing in a public place. My precious jersey, which I wore for the first time, was at its worst. Don't worry; she later bumped into the door frame for her own room, and I no longer felt upset over what she did. She is one very interesting character, but if you ever meet her, be careful; she might either fall or make you drop by making you laugh too much. Anyway, the day was hectic and tiring, and finally, our room's fan got cleaned as well, which is great news. I also placed an order for a TAPMI hoodie. One is cream, and the navy blue is the zipper version. Tomorrow is a Monday, so I need to get a good amount of rest.

15th January' 2024

It was a Monday, but our first session was at a time different than 10:15 AM; instead, we had our first class at 11:45 AM. I woke up around 9 AM and had my breakfast, then got ready and left for class. The first class was Scientific Thinking, where ma'amMa'am taught us the basics like what Science is, what knowledge is, and all. I finally figured out how to get my marks for class participation by spewing scientific possibilities that I studied and read about in my older grades. Like I literally said, the earth would stop rotating, and then the sun could not rise. It was a crazy statement that led to many debates, and the class soon became chaotic. Anyways, our next session was Culture and Context, and this was going to be taught to us by Professor Raghu Menon, who was also our Anthropology professor from the previous semester. He explained to us how this would be much more mythological and based on Indian text and context class. He said we would have more audio and visual-based learning as well. This is a project-based course, and he isn't sure if we have a midterm, but for sure, we do not have an end semester for this course. He said he would clarify this by the end of this week; he made watch a movie called "Jhadu Katha." We will be discussing this in the next class. The last session for the day was Financial Accounting, and sir continued to make us solve questions based on FIFO, LIFO, and Weighted Average, and he left us 7-8 minutes early. He told us that if he is given the last session, the evening session from 4 PM to 5:15 PM, he usually leaves his class 7-8 minutes early. Our class applauded his thinking without any hesitation. Once we were done, I finally purchased notebooks for this semester. I was living over my previous batch of books, which was becoming one hell of a headache, but now that problem was out, which for sure made life easier than ever. Tomorrow, we have three sessions, and it starts from the morning session; hence, I need sleep. Toddles people.

16th January'2024

Today, we have only two sessions. The first one is mathematics, and Ma'am continued with the previous topic and gave us different insights and ways of solving matrices. The next session was Financial Accounting, where sir taught us how to solve periodic inventory problems using LIFO, FIFO, and Weighted Average. He also taught us how to analyze and give statements for the same in case of an increase or decrease in the prices of purchases. We were also informed by our Sports Captains that today, our girls' basketball team has their first match against PGDM 2 BKFS. Our team played very well and broke TAPMI's 42-year legacy and scored 65 to 0. It was an absolutely thrilling match, and Diva was our MVP with 38 points. It was a crazy night and super fun. Once we reached our hostel, we were absolutely drained and exhausted from all the cheering and TAPMI's never-ending slope.

17th January 2024

Today, we have three sessions, and the first one is Business Mathematics; today, ma'am started determinants and taught us its basics and operations. The next session was Scientific Thinking, where Ma'am taught us more about topics like knowledge, how we define knowledge, and under what parameters we verify that something is knowledge. The last session was Foundations of Psychology, where Sir taught us different research methods in Psychology by giving us problems to solve. It was a fun and interactive class. Today, we don't have any SPEED matches, but tomorrow is the Girl team's match. Get some popcorn cause I'm confident that they'll slay.

18th January 2024

It is a holiday today for some government reasons or something, not for some festival. I woke up early, had my breakfast, studied a little bit of economics, and procrastinated for a while. Then, our girls' basketball team had their match against Twornados, and they played amazingly well. It was a good competition. We won by 38-5, and once again, our MVP was Diva; I'm telling you she ain't a joke on the field and is one cool and fiery captain. Off-field, she is the total opposite of that. She is a cutie and very lovable. We were a little late today and past our curfew, but we convinced the warden and finally went in and rested.

19th January 2024

We initially had four classes, but then the first session was canceled, and now we have only three sessions, and they started at 11:45 AM. The first class was Financial Accounting, in which Sir continued to teach us about the difference between service and merchandising companies. And how inventory systems of periodic and perpetual systems work. The next session was Culture and Context, where sir gave us the introduction to Indian Philosophy and boy, this ain't my cup of tea. I miss anthropology, and what's worse is that sir remembers me and how I liked anthropology last semester and has high hopes for my class participation, but nothing genuinely comes out of my head, which I can tell and get some points for. It was a very conflicting class for me. The last session was Foundations of Psychology, and sir continued with the previous topic of research methods and taught us a few more methods. Today we had our boys' basketball team's first match, they played against Broke Bankers, and damn, it was one very competitive and heated match. We lost in the last quarter to a close margin of 24-31. But the team played very well, and we were very proud of them. Once we were back, we chatted for a while. Also, I forgot to mention that I also got my room painted, and cleaning and setting up again was very tiring. The ZOLO team did indeed help with the room, but the setup was tiring. After that, once I came back after the match, my room smelled like paint, and it was so annoying.

CHAPTER THREE

New trend, ATHARVA

20th January 2024

Today is a third Saturday and a holiday. I woke up a little early and had my breakfast. I forgot to mention two days ago, Bishakha and I went to Walmart after a long while. We shopped there and at Max, Style Union, and Zudio. Anyways, back to Saturday, today is the first day of Atharva. Atharva is a cultural fest at TAPMI, and people from many different places and institutes participate. They not only have cultural activities but also Management Fest. We have Battle of Bands and Vibes. In Vibes, we had a few of our classmates and students of MIT's DOC (Department of Commerce) participating as well. The dance by them was terrific, but TAPMI's Roots and Rhythm was an amazing team; I am telling you, when we had our dance battle, I was seriously cheering for them over our own team. They were absolutely a blessing to the eyes, and their moves were genuinely mesmerizing. But our team was also amazing and fought very well. Although we lost, it was a match worth watching. Once we were back, it was way beyond the final curfew as well, and we were reprimanded by our warden for being late. It was one tiring argument, and we finally calmed her down by talking to her. Harsh, our logistics representative, also spoke to her. Finally,

Sneha and I went back up; she was also there, convincing the warden not to give us late entry as it was an official TAPMI event. Anyhow, tomorrow we also have Atharva and our class's girls taking part in their fashion show known as Libas. I have to help them get ready, so it's better for me to get some sleep.

21st January' 2024

On the last day of Atharva, I woke up a little late and had brunch directly. It was Chicken Biryani, which was heavenly as I was having it after a long while. Then, once I came back, I did the eye makeup of 4-5 people and finally got ready myself. We left for Libas in the evening around 5:15 PM. There were at least 2 hours till Libas started, so me and my friends went down towards the food festival to have something till then. I had a potato twister and then got face painting from TAPMI's Art Club. She made a beautiful butterfly and hearts under my eyes. It was so lovely. Then we went back to watch Libas. Most of the teams were great, and our class did well despite a few formation mistakes. But one team from a fashion forum from a different college was fantastic. They were super awesome, and the performance was eye-catching that night. They only won Libas as well. After this, we had the Pro show or the DJ night. It was a super awesome and thrilling evening at TAPMI. We all danced until we were dead tired and finally left for our hostel; oh, another thing, yesterday I was wearing heels, but as we were already late, we had run up the TAPMI slopes. It was almost impossible for me to run up that terrible slope in heels, so I ran barefoot, and my feet were dead later. So, dear TAPMI, please renovate and make your roads better for the sake of our legs; otherwise, I love you. Back to the topic, we were back and super tired. I couldn't wait to sleep until I realized that tomorrow was Financial Accounting class, and I had not completed my homework. Sneha and I gave each other company and stayed awake until 2 in the morning doing Accounts homework. I was dead after that; I have never fallen asleep so fast as I did today.

CHAPTER FOUR

Lessons Beyond the Lecture Halls

22nd January' 2024

Today, I nearly managed to make it in time for breakfast; I was sleep-deprived trying to finish the Accounts home task. The first session was Financial Accounting, where after waiting for Sir for 45 minutes, we realized he was not going to be coming today. As I had free time, I spoke to Prof Vijay Victor, who taught me economics in the previous session. Well, he couldn't increase my marks but told me to keep practicing for the makeup exam. As he would be leaving within a week, he also suggested that if I have any queries, I contact him by then. The next session was Scientific Thinking, where Ma'am taught us about ontology and epistemology. And gave a brief introduction to Induction and Deduction. After this, we had our FAS meeting with our mentors. They first reprimanded us for not sending them the minutes of the meeting. Then, we discussed our queries and finally wrapped up the meeting. The last session was Culture and Context, where Sir continued with Indian Philosophy. Well, once the day was over, I was exhausted and didn't want to do anything else.

23rd January' 2024

Today is our first session by Prof Prasanth Sharma for Scientific Thinking. He is a visiting faculty member from O.P. Jindal Global University and is the associate professor and associate dean of the Jindal School of Banking and Finance. He is one fantastic teacher. He uses managerial applications not only from the real world but also from our academia, making the class very engaging and interesting to listen to. Today was more of an Introductory class and basics of Science and Knowledge. The last session was Foundations of Psychology, where Sir taught us about neurons and their processes. About neurotransmitters and their composition and usage. It was like a recap class of my 11th, so I was doing perfectly fine, but my other batchmates were finding it difficult to keep up with the class, it makes sense Science is not easy, and that is what we also go through during the commerce-related subjects. So, we both know the feeling and empathize with each other. Well, just like they help us study, we will do the same. Today is the girls's Basketball Semi-finals. We went there around 6:30 PM, and just 10 minutes before the match, we found out that the other team had given us a "bye," which meant they forfeited before the match. We went directly into finals; our players were a little sad as they were completely prepared for the match, but it ended like this. Anyway, a few of them were also injured, so it's a good rest for them. Tomorrow is our final, and we will win for sure. Our girls have practiced very hard for this, and of course, their efforts will not be in vain.

24th January 2024

Again, we have two continuous sessions for Scientific Thinking by Prof Prasanth as he needs to go back. He taught us time paradigms of Science and explained to us our assignment and how we will be graded. I'll explain that later when I start working on it. The next session was Financial Accounting, where sir gave us handouts to solve in the class and made us revise old concepts as well. The last session was Business Mathematics, where Ma'am taught us how to solve determinants in different ways. After solving a few more problems, she called it a day. Today is the Basketball Finals for Girls. We won 38-03, and even our sledding was creative, where our class boys brought buckets from their hostels and asked the opponent to shoot in the bucket instead of the basket. Every time out, they would shoot a ball inside the basket and go crazy. It was a very fun match to watch. The girls played well and won without leaving any crumbs behind. It was one ecstatic and thrilling day for our class.

25th January 2024

Today, we had our fun activity managed by our fun manager. It is trekking at Nethravati Peak of Chikkmanglore. We left at 4:45 AM in the morning and reached the homestay at 8 AM. After breakfast, around 9:30 AM, we left for the mountain on jeeps. The jeep ride was thrilling and super fun, but the same couldn't be said for trekking from my side, at least. It was so tiring and exhausting that I went swearing half the way. No, no, the entire trek, I just swore my way up. I didn't even stop around professors; I was done. Hadn't it been for one guide from Mt.Kinetics, whose name is Benson Dsouza, I wouldn't have made it up. I slipped so many times, and I was dead exhausted. I am telling you, never in my life will I ever trek. I am that done with trekking. Thank goodness tomorrow is a holiday for Republic Day. The first thing I did after coming back was meet my Physiotherapist, Rishbha, who, at this point, is just my bestie. She suggested some rest and application of muscle relief sprays like Move or Volini. I chatted or, in a clearer fashion, gossiped with her until 1:30 AM, and then my body pain and knee pain knocked me out.

26th January 2024

It is Republic Day, but I could not attend the parade by TAPMI and my batchmates because the pain from yesterday's trek was killing me. Once I woke up and had brunch, I did my laundry and chatted for a long time with Mithra and Sneha. Then we went down to the canteen for our hi-tea and then did some snack shopping and then came back to our rooms. I procrastinated for a while and then went for dinner. After dinner, we couldn't walk for long as our body pain was killing us. We went to bed early as we had class tomorrow and Quiz On The Beach as well. It is a flagship event of TAPMI that is organized on a beach. Anyway, all that for tomorrow, now it is time to sleep.

27th January 2024

Today, we have only two lectures, both of which are on microeconomics by a visiting faculty member who was once a part of the TAPMI family. He is a great teacher with a fantastic grasp of the subject and language. It was just an introductory session today, but it was not at all boring. After this, we had a quiz on the beach, and we left on one cramped and small bus to Malpe. It was scorching hot, but the quiz was fun. We had a few audience questions as well, but it was pretty informative. We had our dinner at TAPMI's Student Centre and then came back to our hostel. Although tomorrow is a Sunday, we have Economics class, and we need to somehow live through it. On that note, I better get some sleep.

28th January 2024

It was the first Sunday that I had gotten up for class; after breakfast and getting ready, we left for our class. Sir, first off, apologize to us, as we have to attend classes on Sunday. He is a really good human being and an amazing teacher. He taught us about Equilibrium and a little bit of comparative statistics. After we were back, I was exhausted and took a quick nap. Once I woke up, I finished the previous FAS meeting minutes and then had my dinner. You know I learned today that we could purchase extra sales food at the canteen using the canteen card. I didn't know that I had purchased it previously times using my own cash. All that money that I could have invested in something went down the drain like that. Anyway, I am not gonna repeat that again. Tomorrow is Monday, and tomorrow we also have class. When will I ever have a holiday?

29th January 2024

Today, we have four classes; we first had two classes in Microeconomics, where Sir continued with Equilibrium and elasticity. He then informed us that he would again be coming sometime in mid-February and that till then, we should keep practicing to improve. The next session was

Sustainability, Responsibility, and Managerial Ethics, which was going to be taught to us by Professor Purnima; she is super cool and amazing. Very chill and just a little strict about timings. But I am still a great fan of her and her teaching. For our first session, she played a documentary about the planet Earth called "A Life On Our Planet." Of course, we could not finish the entire documentary at once, but it was a beautifully and intelligently created documentary. It did not conceive any facts and spoke the truth about human activities towards the planet, be they good or bad. The last session was supposed to be Culture and Context, but suddenly, it was changed to Foundations of Psychology. It was an unexpected class for both the professor as well as the students. Sir completed the biological aspect of the brain that is used while studying psychology. Once we were back at the hostel after class, I did not do anything productive. I discussed IPM Diaries - Vol 01 with my father and then uploaded it for review. It was one tiring day, and I bid goodbye to it soon.

30th January 2024

We had only one class today, and it was Mathematics; ma'am taught us the basics of calculus, and I was not that much into the class as I was exhausted; my weekends went into attending economics classes. Nothing towards sir. It's just my body is still not used to this, and the exhaustion is just killing me. Once the class was over, I came back and rested. I then researched my scientific thinking assignment's research paper. I am going to do the assignment in the Psychology domain, but as I do not have any specific topic that I want to read about, it is a little more time-consuming and energy-draining.

31ˢᵗ January 2024

Today, we have two sessions; the first session was Sustainability, Responsibility and Managerial Ethics, where first we completed the documentary that we were watching, then Purnima, oh yeah, she prefers to either be called by her first name or as Prof, told us certain key terms to be aware of while discussing the topic of sustainability like El Lino, La Lina, Substantial farming, global warming and so on. It was an amazing class and probably the best course being taught to us by one of the best professors I have come across. The next session was Business Mathematics, where Ma'am explained one complex topic that got the entire class confused. She is trying to simplify it, and once she teaches us that way, I will let you know what she taught. But apart from that, ma'am takes her feedback seriously and works very well on it. She is the perfect example of how we must take all our feedback, be it negative or positive, and work on it to become not only better managers but even better human beings.

February 01ˢᵗ 2024

Today is the last class for inventory management in Financial Accounting. Sir recapped all the topics he covered in this class and held a doubt clarification session; he also made us solve a few questions for a better understanding of the topic. The next session was Culture and Context, where Sir spoke in depth about the Origins of Caste in Indian Philosophy and Buddhism, as well as its beliefs. After this class, we went back to our hostels. We decided to goof around for a while before doing anything productive.

February 02nd 2024

The first session today was Culture and Context, but as Sir had a conference to attend instead, he gave an assignment, which was to write a summary of chapters 3 and 4 after either listening to its podcast or reading the chapters. We were asked to do this assignment in our previous anthropology groups of the first semester, which constituted me, Mithra, Sai, Sapta, and Shrinidhi. We first divided our work and got to work. The next session was Foundations of Psychology by Prof Manoj; he taught us Consciousness and gave a brief introduction to Sleep. I love this subject, so it was a wonderful class. This was the last session; once we were back at our hostels, we first finished our assignment and mailed it, Sir, then we chatted about spooky and scary stories, which are not for the light-hearted. And we were also suddenly informed that the girl's throwball match would be scheduled for tomorrow. And it suddenly became a crazy and hectic night. We all went to bed with so much to intake in one night.

February 03rd 2024

Our first session was Business Mathematics, which was a doubt clarification and practice session; we all sat down and worked on sums and asked ma'am if we had any doubts. The next session was Financial Accounting, where Sir started the new chapter about Fraud and explained the basic concepts. It was pretty theoretical, but we somehow survived, thanks to Sir's examples and class engagement. The last session was Culture and Context, where he first acknowledged our assignment submission despite our hectic schedule. I explained more about caste and our beliefs based on the Upanishads. After this session, we learned that the throw ball match scheduled for girls was not going to happen as the opposite team gave us a "bye." Which meant our team won the first round even without playing it. Once we were back after resting, I went and met a friend and ate at Polar Bear. Well, at least I ended the day on a sweeter note.

February 04th 2024

Today is Sunday, and I have no class, but I can peacefully rest. I woke up in the afternoon and had brunch directly; after that, I worked a little bit on my scientific thinking assignment and studied a little bit of Economics for my makeup exam. Then, I chatted with Diva, Sneha, and Mithra. At the end of the day, I was reminded of how I had class tomorrow again and that I was so done with my life.

CHAPTER FIVE

Workshop that Shaped Perspectives

February 05^{th,} 2024

It is Monday, and the first session is Scientific Thinking by Prof Manoj; he has an interesting way of giving us marks for class participation; he gives us a tiny note with marks and his sign for any valuable addition to our class discussion. We must return this to him at the end of the class with our names on it so he can add it to our class participation category. But I was not feeling well today from the moment I woke up. I somehow survived Financial Accounting class while feeling awful on the inside. My batchmate Diva suggested that it might be a gastric problem, and Ayush offered me digene, which helped, but as I was already not able to concentrate, I went back to the hostel after the second session only. I came back, had lunch, and then slept for a good 3-4 hours, and I was then feeling much better. I missed our class boy's first football match, and it turned out that they played better than everyone expected and even won. It was a super exciting match that I missed, but it is suitable as I can attend the next one.

February 06th 2024

Today, I felt much better than I did yesterday; our first session was Business Mathematics, where Ma'am continued with differential calculus by teaching essential topics like limits. The next session was Sustainability, Responsibility, and Managerial Ethics, where Prof told us that we need to get comfortable speaking about uncomfortable issues like gender-based inequalities, religion, caste, and so on. It was indeed a very eye-opening and practical class with no sugarcoating. After this, we had our field trip for Scientific Thinking at MAP (Manipal Anatomy and Pathology) Museum; it was beautiful and reminded me of my 12th grade. It was an exciting experience. I helped my friends if I had prior knowledge of what was being displayed. They also preserved the dead bodies of a human and many more human and animal specimens. After this, once I was back, I was exhausted as the day was long. After a short rest, I started revising for the Mathematics quiz, which is tomorrow. Thanks to Bishakha's advice for revising and prepping, the process was much faster and easier. Wish me luck, guys, as mathematics ain't my least favorite subject.

February 07th 2024

First, we had our mathematics quiz, which was pretty good; I guess Bishakha's tip and Ma'am's new way of teaching did pay off. After this, as Ma'am still had some time so, she took a small class on limits, and then it was soon time for the next session, which was Foundations of Psychology, where Ma'am taught us classical conditioning and operational conditioning and made us do fun exercise based on that. It was super fun, and this class was perfect. The next session was Financial Accounting. Sir just continued with Fraud and bank statements, but Bishakha had lots of fun in this session. After this class, we finally went back to our hostels, and I worked some more on my Scientific Thinking assignment. Trust me, it's just annoying and frustrating at this point.

08th February' 2024 – 10th February' 2024

Today, tomorrow, and the day after, we have a workshop known as "Through a Sociological Lens-Decoding the Unspoken Rules that Shape Your World," being conducted by Mr Prabir Bose and Prof Purnima Venkat. During three days of the workshop, we did many different activities, starting from being blindfolded in an obstacle race to Problem Tree, playing with clay, and building blocks. It sounds all fun and cool, but they all had deep messages engraved in them. For starters, on the first day, we spoke about identity and how well we know ourselves, and this activity made me realize that I know myself very well, but it might not necessarily be true. The next day, we spoke about poverty and tried decoding its causes using the problem tree. We learned that there will never be one problem tree that completely covers all its root causes; many root causes in themselves have their own problem tree. On the last day, we spoke and understood how we need to widen our lens to see a problem given in front of us and how we must not only interpret it but how it ended that way as well. We need to know how conformed we are to something and if we need to reform it or transform it. Throughout the three days, I personally learned a lot about myself and my batchmates, about words and their meaning in our lives. How to express and respect the opinions of others and ourselves as well. This workshop was one of the best things we have done this semester so far. Both our facilitators were spectacular and did a great job.

February 11^{th,} 2024

It is a Sunday; I did not do anything special other than work on my assignments and complete certain tasks I have been putting behind. Oh, I forgot to mention, but on February 09th, our girl's Throw ball team had two matches and won them with flying colors and made it all the way to the semi-finals. We are totally going to win the semi-finals and finals, and their efforts will pay off.

February 12^{th,} 2024

Today, we have four sessions, the first one being Sustainability, Responsibility, and Managerial Ethics, where Prof first asked us how we left about our workshop, which was held for the last three days and then taught us megatrends and how fast our world has been changing. The next session was Financial Accounting, where Sir gave an assignment that required solving within our working groups. As I hurt my hand, I couldn't do too much and just solved an Ethics problem and a matching problem. We barely finished it in time and submitted it. LIME, a committee, then came and informed us about Meraki, their most awaited event of the year, and urged us to participate in it. Hopefully, we won't have any exams around that time so we can enjoy ourselves. After lunch, we had Culture and Context, where Sir informed us about an assignment that we needed to work on in our previous groups and present it next week. We divided our work and slowly started working on it. The last session was mathematics, and ma'am continued with differential calculus. It was one long day, and once we were back, I did some work on my Scientific Thinking Project and finally bid the day goodbye.

February 13th 2024

Today, we have only two sessions. The first session was of Foundations of Psychology, where Ma'am first reprimanded all of us for not completing our assigned task and wanted us to finish immediately so that she could start her session. Then, ma'am discussed the elements of operant conditioning and the different styles of learning. It was a fun class with an activity and quiz as well. The session was Mathematics, where ma'am taught us how to solve different differential equation problems using different rules. After this, we had a special workshop on Plagiarism by Prof Ganesh; we learned a lot of new things and important tips not to plagiarise unintentionally and intentionally. After this, we had our boy's football match against BKFS Bulls, and our boys played very well but sadly lost due to penalty shootouts. But nonetheless, they played very well, and it was a match worth watching. After this, once we were back, we were tired. I didn't want to do anything, but then again, I had to do some of my Scientific Thinking Assignments. After this, I went to bed.

CHAPTER SIX

The Art of Juggling Responsibilities

February 14th 2024

Today is February 14th, and no, I don't have any special romantic plans, but I am going out to have dinner with my friends. Anyways, the first session was Financial Accounting, where Sir started a new chapter on Receivables, Bad debts, and Interest Revenues. It was a basic class that taught us important terminologies and explained their usage. The next session was Business Mathematics, where ma'am finally completed explaining and solving all basic rule-based differentiations. After this, we had Sustainability, Responsibility, and Managerial Ethics, where she made us do a small experiment and then explained to us the five capital models, which are Natural Capital, Physical Capital, Financial Capital, Human Capital, and Social Capital. In her opinion, even Tech Capital should be one of them. After this, we went back to our hostels. I first rested for a while, then got up and finished my Scientific Thinking Project, and then my friends and I got ready and went out for dinner. It was a fun and nice way to end the day; it was chaotic and fun, and the food was amazing.

February 15th 2024

Today, we have four sessions, the first one being Scientific Thinking, where we discussed Pseudoscience, and it was an interesting discussion. The next session was Culture and Context, where Sir asked for our updates on the assignment and left the class to work and finish the assignment. In the same time period, I also submitted my Scientific Thinking Assignment, and then it was time for lunch. After lunch, we had Financial Accounting, where Sir continued with the previous topic and informed us that in the next class, he would solve problems. The last session was Mathematics, and we started with Applications of Differential Calculus. Finally, the long and exhausting day was over, and tomorrow, we had no sessions. Our class boys had their first Volleyball match, which they lost, but it's okay; there will always be a next time. Mithra and I did some shopping and were done with the day.

February 16th 2024

Today, I woke up a little late and went to Butterfly for breakfast. Once I was done, I went to Kasturba and showed my eye. It turns out I have dry eye and need to put on eye drops for a month and four times a day. After this, I packed my lunch and went back to the hostel. Later in the evening, Mithra and I went to the Parlor and got some self-care done. After this, we had rolls and this really yummy Manchurian fried rice from Boda Sheera, which was heavenly. Today, interestingly, was a self-care day. I realized how important it is to take care of one's physical and mental health and that I should do this every once in a while.

February 17^{th,} 2024

Today is a holiday on account of the third Saturday. I slept through the breakfast and directly had brunch. Then, I worked on my part for the Culture Context report. I also worked on my Scientific Thinking Presentation, which was required for class on Monday.

February 18^{th,} 2024

It was Sunday today, and it was the same story as every Sunday: sleeping through breakfast, directly having brunch, and then finishing all the work. We have started compiling our Culture and Context Report, which is due tomorrow afternoon. And then, after spending some time with friends and goofing around, my precious holiday weekend was over.

February 19^{th,} 2024

Today, I finished presenting my Scientific Thinking Presentation on the Origins of Specific Phobias, and then our team presented a Culture and Context Report, which went very well. I answered all the questions asked of me clearly and confidently, and so did my team. The last session was Business Mathematics, where ma'am taught us one last application on differentiation, which we called a day. Once I was back, I realized I had a really long week ahead with even our Sunday class. Anyway, I don't have any home tasks or presentations for tomorrow's classes, so I went to bed early.

February 20ᵗʰ' 2024

The first two sessions were Scientific Thinking, where the professor completed the remaining presentations and then taught us our final topics from his side. It was his last class with us today, but nonetheless, he is a great teacher; we learned to view many things differently, and it was a good experience. After this, we had Financial Accounting, where Sir gave us handouts to solve. This chapter is not the easiest, so it took us an entire 75-minute session to solve just three problems. The last session was Sustainability, Responsibility, and Managerial Ethics, where we all suffered in the class as the air conditioner was not working, and it was super hot, like gosh; it was too hot. So, she asked Harshitaa to check if the Bloomberg lab was free, and it was free. For the first time, we had a class in Bloomberg lab, and it was not for Accounts but for this class. Anyways, she taught us Stakeholder Mapping and gave us an assignment to work on. We had to visit any small shop around us and make the map a stakeholder mapping for them. It was still a very fun class.

February 21ˢᵗ' 2024

The first session was Business Mathematics, where ma'am kept this class for doubt clarification and practice for the term, which is two days from now. After this, we had three sessions of Design Thinking, and the first session was pure chaos as we were asked to build the longest free-standing tower using balloons. We spent too much time thinking and, in the end, partnered up with another team to finish it. There was so much noise, and it was super fun.

After this, in the next session, he gave us a rough idea about how this course is structured and how he wants to deliver it to us. Then we had the highlight of the day, the introduce yourself part. I was the first candidate, but funnily enough, I got weird nicknames like hybrid species. I am Bengali, and I was born and brought up in Bangalore. There was too much of chaos in class once they heard this special nickname. But I am telling this was one of the craziest classes I have attended in a while. Once we were back at the hostel after class, I revised a little bit of Mathematics for the Mid-term and fell asleep.

February 22nd, 2024

Today, we once again started off with Mathematics, which was a practice class for the midterm only. Then we had Financial Accounting, where Sir once again explained bad debts and solved two more problems. We were now supposed to have Culture and Context, but it was moved to Monday; after one session gap, we had Foundations of Psychology, where Sir completed Sleep and its Disorders. It was a super fun class and a mind-opener sort. We learned so much more about our precious Sleep, who is, at this point, my soulmate that I really cannot live without. Once we came back to the hostel, I revised for the Mathematics exam and wished to pass it tomorrow.

February 23rd, 2024

The first two sessions were Microeconomics, where Sir started with Equilibrium, Elasticity, and Comparative statistics and then continued with Consumer Behaviour. After this, we had our Mathematics Mid-term exam, which went well. After we came back to the hostel, within an hour or so, we left again for TAPMI as we had Veloura, a Fashion event where six of our batchmates had taken part. The event was great, and our batchmates also did very well; the crowd was small. The last event was the performance from TAPMI's band YTBN, which literally means, Yet To Be Named. They were fire-like spectacular performances worth watching. We were back at 11:15 PM and then went and prepared for the Microeconomics quiz, which was tomorrow. I wish you luck cause my relationship with Economics has been interesting.

CHAPTER SEVEN

Notes, Nonsense and Naptime

February 24th 2024

Today, we had three Microeconomics sessions. In the first 15 minutes, we had our quiz, which was good, and then Sir taught us the Price Consumption Curve, Income Consumption Curve, Producer surplus, and Consumer Surplus. Once we came back, we went to MIC (Manipal Institute of Communication) to attend Namma Santhe, which Prof Purnima had asked us to attend. We also met her, and it was a great fest; I got a henna tattoo with my rabbit babies as an inspiration, ate good food, and purchased cute things and a snake ring. That ring is super cool, I am telling you. But on the way to the fest, one nightmare took place: I stepped on Cow dung wearing white crocs. It's such a nightmare. It was one disgusting event, and I don't ever want to live through it. Ew, thinking about it makes my stomach feel weird. Anyway, other than that, the day was nice and fun.

February 25th 2024

It is a Sunday today, but today I also have a class that has two microeconomics sessions. We solved multiple numerals, and he asked us to keep practicing to improve ourselves before the mid-term examination. He also informed us that he would be back in the last week of March for class, and it will be an entire week of microeconomics. One of these sessions will have our Mid-term Examination. He left us early, and then once we were back, I was exhausted and rested early.

February 26th 2024

The first session today was Culture and Context, where Sir finished the remaining presentations and then asked each team a couple of questions. The next session was Foundations of Psychology, where Sir informed us that we would have our quiz on the first class scheduled in March; he completed Consciousness, and the next session was Business Mathematics, where Ma'am started Integration. The last session was once again Culture and Context, and now Sir taught us about the different divisions of historical periods and the different forms of political rules that existed during those periods. Once we were back, I prepared a little bit for our Quiz on Financial Accounting on February 29th.

February 27th 2024

Today, our first session was Financial Accounting, and Sir taught us the remaining few problems from the handouts he had given to us and completed them. The next class was Business Mathematics, where Ma'am continued with yesterday's topic only. The last class was Foundations of Psychology, and Sir started with Perception. After this, we went back to the hostel and came back again to campus as it was the first day of WAVES, and our class won Comic Stan, whose members were Akshay, Uttkarsh, and Sanidhya. They got the topic of Wedding Proposal Gone Wrong, and after 2 minutes of discussion, they performed their impromptu act and won our judge, Prof Aparna Bhat's heart; she was our English Language and Literature Professor from last semester. We also took part in Hunger Games, but sadly, we did not win. However, our class had lots of fun.

February 28th‘ 2024

Mathematics, we have so many sessions continuously with ma'am that she might as well start living with us in our hostels. The first session, you guessed it right, is Business Mathematics, and ma'am is still teaching and making us practice Integration. The next session was Sustainability, Responsibility, and Managerial Ethics, where we started working on our Stakeholder Mapping team project; my team consisted of me, Mithra, Bishakha, Sneha, and Harshitaa. Our business of interest is Butterfly Cafe, which is an eatery that is very close to our hostel. The last session was Culture and Context, in which Sir continued to elaborate on the political changes from 1000 BCE to 100 BCE. After this, we had our finals of Throwball against the Maestros, which we lost, but by a very close margin; it was a wonderful match and worth watching. After this I and my friends for the first time saw the volleyball match of Maestros and damn, they were so good we totally were in awe. Then WAVES Day-02 started, and today, we took part in Rangmanch and came third. We had a phenomenal performance, but we couldn't be first as we had extended the time limit way too much. The next event was Symphony, where we came second overall. It was a day filled with wins. After we returned back to the hostel, I immediately sat to revise for the Financial Accounting quiz, which is tomorrow. Wish me luck cause lately, my luck with accounts could have been better than it was last semester.

February 29th ' 2024

The extra day of the year is February 29th. The first session was Business Mathematics, and Ma'am started Applications of Integrals, and then the next session was Scientific Thinking, where we continued with Parapsychology and completed our discussion with it. The next session was our quiz, which was really awful; I did terribly, but I did not have enough time to be upset as tomorrow is my Foundations of Psychology quiz. The last session was Culture and Context, where Sir gave us a recap to study before mid-term and gave us a tiny revision of all the topics he discussed. Today is the last day of WAVES, and we took part in the last event, Dance Pe Chance. Although we didn't win, it was a thrilling and amazing event to watch. I went back with Harshitaa before the DJ night as I wanted to revise for the Psychology quiz, which is tomorrow. We were the first runner-up of WAVES, and it was amazing.

01st March 2024

We have only two sessions today after a long time. The first session was Foundations of Psychology, where we first had our quiz, which went well, and then Sir continued with

Perception. The next session was Business Mathematics, and we continued with the previous topic. Once we were back, I rested for a while and then went out for a little while. We discussed our SRME project a little by calling the Owner of Butterfly and clarifying our queries.

02nd March 2024

The first session was Sustainability, Responsibility, and Managerial Ethics, where we continued with our chart making, And the last session was Business Mathematics and ma'am continued with the Application of Integrals. After this, we returned to our rooms, and then after a while, we left for campus again as we had the ending ceremony of SPEED, which we had won with 6100 points, setting a new record. We received our trophy with utmost pride and celebrated to our heart's content. After this, Harshitaa gave us a treat as she and her team won two competitions. It was an amazing way to end the day.

03rd March' 2024

Today is finally a Sunday when I can rest. I woke up and had brunch. After this, I had some work, which I finished, and then I suddenly heard in the evening from Tharun that we were going to Bangalore tomorrow evening as there was a photo shoot that we needed to attend on the Bangalore campus. Only six of us, which included me, Sneha, Tharun, Ayush, and two more people, have yet to be told that the previous candidates cannot come as they are busy. Crazy stuff, and after that, our team practiced for our SRME presentation tomorrow, and I am going to act as the Owner. It will be one iconic presentation that I will be delivering with them this Semester.

CHAPTER EIGHT

Start of the Project Era

04th March 2024

Today, we have only two sessions, the first one being Culture and Context, where Sir taught how Chandra Gupta expanded his empire and how to go about after his demise. He also asked us if he had any queries about the midterm, which is on this Friday. The next session was our presentation session, where my part was to role-play Vinayak Kamath, the Owner of Butterfly Cafe, and to enact the discussion our team had with him and Bishakha. Sneha, Mithra, and Harshitaa explained other topics. Ma'am initially didn't have any questions to ask, and later on, whatever question was asked to us by Ma'am and my batch mates, we answered them with confidence. After this, we came back to our hostels after having lunch; Sneha accompanied me to KMC as I had pain in my tooth, which is my wisdom tooth, for about a week. After an x-ray, I was informed that the wisdom tooth on my right side was decaying and that they needed to extract it. I told them that this Friday was the only possible day for this, and they also reassured me that it was safe as the moment I stepped in, everyone just instinctively knew that I was scared. I am really scared of dentists, but I need to take care of my tooth, or it will be a problem for me only later. This week, they will extract my right wisdom tooth, and next week, they will extract my left wisdom tooth, which is strangely in a sleeping position. However, as it is not an impending problem at the moment, they will first only extract the right wisdom tooth. After this, we returned to having ice cream. I first packed my suitcase and then did my laundry and washed my hair, which I couldn't do in the morning. Sadly, Sneha's formal jacket caught fungus, and she spent a lot of time looking for another alternative. After this, we had some issues with our hostel leave, which we fixed with the help of Prof Vishnu, Prof Krishna Prasad, and Parimala Ma'am. After this, all that remained was our bus trip. I, like a dumb and irresponsible lid, forgot my phone charger and toothbrush. Well, for the phone charger, I can use Sneha's, but I had to buy one for the toothbrush. All right, people need to wake up early tomorrow, toddlers.

05th March 2024

It was one chaotic day; the photo shoot was very tiring; we had to wear formal clothes, change into comfy clothes, and then wear formal clothes again. Like my gosh, in that heat, moving around like a bunch of lost sheep, man, don't even get me started on how frustrating that was. First off, upon reaching Bangalore, only our cab guy was lost, not once but twice. That was the beginning of us being lost throughout the day. We faked and laughed so much that, at some point, my gum started drying up. The campus overall is pretty, and so is the hostel, but I still personally prefer my hostel and campus. One is because I am familiar, and the second is because I am more comfortable there. Later, we also met the dean of the TAPMI Bangalore campus; he was a really nice and polite guy. Very humble from beginning to end, and even offered us tea or coffee. Funnily, I don't drink either, but it was a very kind and nice gesture. After this, I met my sister and mother, who bought me food and a few accessories. After this, we packed again and left for our bus. We chatted for a while on the bus, which was not the greatest for sure, but whatever. Then we went to bed as we had to wake up early tomorrow.

06th March 2024

We reached Manipal around 8:30 AM; our first session was empty, so we had enough time to unpack, have breakfast, and then get ready for class after a nice warm bath. Our first session was Foundations of Psychology, where we were asked to give Prof an update on how our project has been proceeding. I gave an impromptu presentation with Mithra and Harrsh. At this point, we have mastered impromptu presentations. Ma'am was happy with our updates and wished us good luck with our project. The next session was Design Thinking, another chaotic and fun class. We drew portraits of each other, and I learned how bad I sucked at drawing; I felt very bad for my muse Bishakha, but Bishakha and Mithra are phenomenal artists. Mithra drew a very similar portrait of mine. Like, damn, gurl, you are too good. And Bishakha was also no joke, and I turned this poor kid into a joke by drawing such a terrible portrait. But, it is something to laugh at later. Then we watched a TED Talk by Tim Brown, who is the author of the text we will be using for this course. Nonetheless, it was one chaotic and fun class. After this, once I got back, I rested early as the traveling had sucked my life out.

07th March 2024

Today, we have three sessions, the first one being Scientific Thinking, where we discussed sociology and people's views on it. Society and Science, Religion and Science, and so on. The next session was Sustainability, Responsibility, and Managerial Ethics, where we continued with presentations. The last session was Financial Accounting, and Sir, let us prepare for our mid-Sem exam for Culture and Context. He also informed us that he would take an extra class and compensate for this one later. The exam went well, and I was so relaxed after this was over. After this, we came back to the hostel. I had whatever I wanted during dinner as tomorrow is my wisdom tooth removal, after which, for a while, I will not be able to have any good food. After this, I went to bed as my tooth extraction was in the morning.

08th March 2024

Today, I did not attend any class; I had my right wisdom tooth extracted and did not pain much as I was under anesthesia; my left tooth will be in April. Anyway, I started hating ice cream as I had over ten mini tubs, and that was way too much of sweet for me. I do not have a sweet tooth, so it made it worse. But that was not the worst thing cause now the right side of my face was square. Wow, man, I looked like a unique shape, no kidding. Anyway, I am too tired. I shall once again sleep early.

09th March 2024

I went to class looking like a half square, the first session being sustainability, responsibility, and managerial ethics, where we completed all the presentations. Then, the professor taught us how to identify stakeholders based on four factors that may not remain constant and can change. In the last session, Financial Accounting and Sir started a new chapter. Once we were back, I had ice cream again, and then at night, I had soup, which was okay, but I was still a square.

10th March 2024

It is Sunday, and I could not have biryani because of my tooth removal. I had soup—and then ice cream. And then again, once in the evening, I went and had ice cream. For dinner, I had pasta; it was soft and easy to eat but took a while as I could chew only from one side. Anyway, I have classes tomorrow and am so unhappy that I have to wake up early. Alright then, toddles peep!

11th March 2024

Today is Psychology for us as we have two sessions of it. The first session, as you can guess, is Foundations of Psychology, but by Vidya ma'am. She taught us Erik Erikson's Psychosocial Developmental theory. And she also gave us a mini quiz on that to check our understanding. I actually really like this thing she does of testing us on how much we understood cause then it becomes easier for us to understand the concepts and to see where improvement is required. Then we had Culture and Context, where Sir explained to us our new project and how we needed to go about it. It was about forming the laws of an ideal state by using the principles of Atharshastra, which was written by Kautilya. It is an interesting but complex project. After clarifying our doubts, Sir left us early. For lunch, I went to the Student Centre with my friends as I could notneed solid food. After this, the last session was Foundations of Psychology, which was now Prof Manoj's class. He started with memory, which we all seem to be bad about. Jokes apart, he taught us different models that tried to explain memory and sensory memory, which he also gave us tiny tests to understand. Once we were back, I rested as I did not have strength in me with the toothache and everything.

12th March 2024

I woke up in the morning looking less square on one side, but there was still a tiny bit of pain remaining. We were informed due to some institutional reasons; our classes would be held in TMA Pai Block's Conference Hall. It is super fun to sit on those rotating chairs and attend classes. The first session was Business mathematics, where ma'am started partial differentiation and made us solve a few sums. The next session was Financial Accounting, where Sir made us solve problems and told us to carry our text to the next session. After this, the first obstacle was the washroom; as we were not familiar with the block, it took us a long time to find the restroom, only to find out that it was out of order, and then we went up one floor and used that restroom. Here, the "we" were initially me, Bishakha, and Mithra, but once we had to go up, Mithra backed off, and it was just the two of us. Then we had our lunch in the student center. The next class was Scientific Thinking, which was chaotic, and I finally got a few points for class participation, thanks to Sir's thinking. We got the glare from the COE office chair for being way too noisy. Well, our class is just wild like that, and we are totally not blaming Sir for being so done with us. After this, we had our FAS meeting and spoke about our concerns, and then we came back to the hostel.

13th March 2024

Today is design thinking day, with three continuous sessions. The first one went in, Sir, telling us how our attention span is so poor and how we do not want to become lazy and regret our life choices later in life. In the next session, he taught us how to problem analysis by observation and interviewing. It was an anthropological interviewing process. We chose T-bites, a food vendor at the Student Centre. In the next session, we told Sir our observations, and he gave us a set of questions to work on and find the answers for during our interview. The last session was Foundations of Psychology, where Ma'am started Piaget's cognitive theory and then continued with the theory of moral theory development. After this, finally, all our classes were over. I watched a few series after a long time as tomorrow we did not have our first class. And we were then retired for the night.

14th March 2024

I missed the canteen's breakfast as I slept through it. I got ready and went to Butterfly for breakfast and found Siddhi and Harshitaa there. The cafe's Owner was also present, so I called Bishakha and told her to get the chart we made for SRME with her and come down. We gave him the chart, and he was very happy. He gave us free mango shakes. Then we went to college, where the first session was Foundations of Psychology, where Sir continued on memory, and then we had Business Mathematics, and ma'am also gave us more sums to solve on partial differentiation. And then, after returning, I had fun and did time pass before I fell asleep.

15th March 2024

Today, we had only three sessions; the first one was Culture and Context. After updating Sir about our team's project, I rushed to Kasturba and got my sutures removed. I learned jaw-opening exercises and came back to class on time. The next session was Business Mathematics, where ma'am started the application of partial differential. Then, the next session was Financial Accounting, where Sir helped us solve textbook problems. After this, we came back to our hostel rooms and did our pending tasks so that we could enjoy our weekend.

16th March 2024

Finally, on a third Saturday, which is off, I spent all the fun and time that I could not spend the past few days. Actually, I kept getting multiple asking me if they could join my Culture and Context group. We refused everyone who asked. We had already divided our work and were almost done. It was an unexpected situation that I had not been through before, but I learned how to deal with it with the help of my group.

CHAPTER NINE

Projects, Presentations, and the Pursuit of Perfection

17th March 2024

Today, I started working on my part of the culture and context project. It was to devise the policies and strategies of our ideal state either by using Arthashastra's principles or by other strategic methods. I had already divided the work amongst my team, which was different from my working group. It has me, of course; Mithra is also there everywhere. At this point, I should have a chapter named under her. There is also Saptarshi, Yogendra, and Shrinidhi, the three boys with whom we have been working together since last Semester and have great teamwork. I finished my work and gave it to my team for review.

18th March 2024

Our first class today was Culture and Context, where Sir started to explain to us a new topic that consisted of ethics in terms of Western and Indian texts. It was a very interesting session where we spoke about topics like lying. Is theft justified, and so on? After this, we had mathematics, and ma'am continued to solve and make us understand more problems under Module 4. The last session was Foundations of Psychology, where ma'am made us do a unique assignment to understand ourselves better. We also wrote compliments for each other, and one of the unique ones was someone wrote that I am an intellect, and that was strange as I had never heard of that. After this class, we came back to our hostel and prepared our report for Culture and Context. We also started working on our presentation, which we will be presenting tomorrow.

19th March 2024

Our first session was again Culture and Context, where we presented. We were very satisfied with our presentation and proud of our team. After this, it was mathematics, and it quickly flew by after solving a few problems. I left after this class to go to Kasturba for my eye checkup and missed Financial Accounting. My power had increased a little, so I went and placed an order for my new glasses, which took a lot of time because I made one wrong choice of asking my family's opinion, who kept changing answers or not agreeing with each other, which made the process longer. Afterward, with the staff's help, I chose my glasses, paid for them, and left to go back to the hostel.

20th March 2024

It is Design Thinking Day; Sir taught us how to conduct anthropological interviews and asked us to go back to our previous business or person that we chose to observe and conduct the interviews. We all went back to the Student Centre, first ate, and then conducted the interview. After this, we discussed our Scientific Thinking presentation ideas and came up with the idea of doing a skit, which was written by Mithra and narrated by her. The actors were Varun and me, and the prop and scenario handlers were Raghav and Gauranshi. After this, we returned to class, and five groups other than ours presented their observations and findings. Once we went back to the hostel, I first started by revising for the Foundations of Psychology mid-semester exam, which was tomorrow, and then worked on our presentation, fixing anything if required and removing unnecessary slides. Sadly, we got a message that one of our teammates could not be present for tomorrow's presentation as he had a personal emergency. We tried to postpone our presentation, which did not work, so we had to update our presentation. I took all his parts, the skit I modified it, and then also worked on his parts and finally went to bed.

21st march 2024

The first two sessions were Scientific Thinking, where we presented our topic, which was the Wheel; we rehearsed only once before performing and did our jobs very well. Many of my peers came up to me and told me how they enjoyed my presentation and how well my team presented; even though there were a few obstacles during our presentation, we somehow overcame them. After this, the next session was Business Mathematics, where ma'am made us solve a few sums, and then she let us study for our Psychology mid-term. Next was the Foundations of Psychology midterm, and I did well; the last question, I wasn't,needed clarification on but I still made use of whatever I could and finished my paper. It was a very long day, and once it was done, I was so tired and ready to sleep.

22nd March 2024

Today, we have three sessions, and the first one begins with Financial Accounting. Sir taught us new concepts like bonds and how to pass entries for them. The next session was initially Culture and Context, which was canceled at the faculty's request. Upon requesting Prof Vidhya to move up her class, she agreed, and then we had the Foundations of Psychology session where Ma'am started the theories of Personality; we started with Freud's Theory of Personality. After this one, we returned, and Sneha packed our bags as we took a bus to catch Bangalore. We were going for the promotional shoot, and this time, there were only four of us: Sneha, Tharun, and Yash. It was a chaotic night as the IPL had also started, and it was a war of nerves between CSK fans Tharun and Yash and RCB fan Sneha. My goodness, they had a great time pulling each other's legs. We tried to go to bed early as we needed to wake up on time for our stop.

23rd March 2024

We reached the Yeshwantpur bus stand at 6 AM in the morning. We then hailed the cab arranged by TAPMI. We were also accompanied by Shiv Kumar Sir. We reached the hostel and then peacefully showered and got ready. Sneha panicked a little as her shirt had crumpled, but we had no choice but for her to wear it, and once I calmed her down, I went to shower. We had a hectic day ahead. I was the first one to record her testimonial, and then I got my montage shots along with Yash. After one eternity's wait, Tharun finally completed his shoot, and we got our group shots. Prof Vishnu, who is our IPM Chair, was also there for the photoshoot; we took photos with him as well, and then he bought me chips and chatted with us for a long time. In the evening after the shoot, I went home and met my bunnies after so long. I honestly missed them so much and was totally delighted to see them. I spoke with family, got group pictures, ate good food, and then finally dropped me off at Yeshwantpur, where a bus would be coming. We left to go back to Manipal, and honestly, everyone was exhausted. They did not talk much and just went to sleep.

24th March 2024

We reached Manipal at 8:45 AM and then quickly got ready and left class. I just attended one class out of two as I was dead tired, and then I went to Lenskart and picked up my new glasses. Once I was back at the hostel, I got my room cleaned, fell asleep, and did not have lunch. Later in the evening, Bishakha gave us her belated birthday treat. Her birthday was on the 23rd, which I and Sneha missed, but I didn't worry; we created a legendary video that she enjoyed thoroughly. It was also a very fun dinner, tasty and appetizing to the soul.

25th March 2024

Today is a holiday for Holi, and I rested through half the day; after this, I had my lunch, and then Mithra taught me Microeconomics as we have it's mid-term soon. After this, I procrastinated and did nonsense to pass the time.

26th March 2024

The first two sessions were Microeconomics, and Sir taught us new topics and then made us practice problems for tomorrow's mid-term. After this, we had Psychology class where Ma'am taught the other theory of Personality, and then we concluded the class with a quiz. After this, we returned back to the hostel and then goofed around for a while. Then I started preparing for the Microeconomics mid-semester exam, and it was not easy, dude, that too when you are not confident in yourself for this subject, but somehow, I just kept going, and it was pretty tiring, but I did not give up as Mithra had put in so much effort so there was no way I could give up easily. Anyways, guys, wish me luck with the paper tomorrow.

27th March 2024

We started the day with our Microeconomics exam, and I gave it my all, but it was challenging, and it was more or less the entire class's opinion on the paper. After this, Sir taught us a few new topics, but clearly, our class needed help to focus because the paper was not easy and had crushed our existence. After this, we returned our SPEED trophy to Sportscom as they were going to give it to a senior of ours who had unfortunately passed away recently. She was an amazing and kind senior, very easy to approach, and all of us loved her. This showed us how to value life more, how unpredictable the future is, and that we should try to live our lives to the fullest while being sensible again. We will always remember her for all the unforgettable memories we shared with her during SPEED.

28th March 2024

We have a guest lecture from Dr Aman Jain, the VP of Corporate HR of Sterling Resorts, who is a very fun and cool guy. He talked about how our own personalities can influence our and others' lives. We attended a very cool and interesting lecture. After this, we had Microeconomics, where Sir explained a little bit of our paper, and then we saw our pathetic marks. Even then, I was happy as whatever I could score was thanks to Mithra's help. Then we had Culture and Context, where Sir completed how many presentations he could, and then again we had a paper discussion for a while on Microeconomics, and then Sir started Perfectly Competitive Markets and continued to explain how much he could before the class ended. After this, we went back to the hostel. I made two new friends thanks to Mithra during dinner, and after chatting for a long, we went to bed. You see, tomorrow is Good Friday, and that's why we remained awake for so long.

29th March 2024

I woke up early as Mithra wanted to go to KMC, but it was closed due to Good Friday; I had breakfast, then chatted for a while, and then went to shower. Again, Mithra tried to go to the gym, which was also closed. To lift her mood, we went to Machali; oh my dawg, I had the best food I had eaten at Manipal. After this, we went to Polarbear and had amazing ice cream treats, clicked a lot of pictures, and then walked back in the heat like two dumb kids. We came back to the hostel, had some more fun, and then studied Financial Accounting. Then, we were exhausted and gave up. We went for dinner and came back and started our second semester of iconic karaoke nights. So today, we went from sad Mithra Day to Happy Mithra Day.

30th March 2024

Today, we had our first-ever panel discussion, and the topic of discussion was Reward and Recognition (R&R) in corporate; our guest lectures were esteemed heads from the corporate world. They gave us new ways to think of R&R and showed us how important it is to have this in the workforce. It was very engaging and mind-opening, but it was too long. I need to work on my attention span on that note. It was Prof Vidhya's last class for us before her retirement, and we will miss her. She was absolutely amazing and made teaching fun. We paid even more attention to her class, and once she was done, we all proudly stood up and clapped and cheered for her and told her how much we loved her and would miss her teachings. After this, we had Sustainability, Responsibility, and Managerial Ethics (SRME), where Prof taught us how to measure the Triple bottom line—and then made us watch a video on Triple Bottom Line. After this, once we were back, we were all very exhausted and just wanted to sleep. Later in the night, we had our Semester awaiting crazy karaoke session. I almost lost my voice and went back to all the singing, which was practically screaming at some point and dancing to our heart's content. I was super exhausted and knocked myself out after this chaotic session.

31st March 2024

It was Sunday, and my routine was not anything new from the usual Sunday routine. I had a pile of diary entries that I had not made, and I had to sit and write them down. My physical age may be 19, but my mental age is over 80 years old. I can hardly remember things and clearly suck at keeping a schedule. I am not the most organized person when it comes to all this. Anyways, tomorrow is April Fools and I hope no one fools me

Late-Night Laments

01st April 2024

We had classes from our second slot, the 11.45 AM slot, so finally, after quickly finishing my shower and breakfast, I and Mothra went to Kasturba. Well, it's a little personal, but we went to the hospital because someone stole my heart. Kidding! I had you in the first half, didn't I? You cannot hold it against me as it's April Fools. We went to Kasturba as Mithra wanted to get a checkup for discomfort that she had been facing for a while. And I, as an amazing friend and human being, accompanied her. Her tests were taking too long, so she sent me off to class, and she came later during lunch break. The first session was Foundations of Psychology, and sir was late as he forgot our classes till the end of this semester were going to be held in TMA Pai, not KK Pai. Sir came running and prayed that he wouldn't make this mistake again. He started a new chapter called Cognition: Thinking, Intelligence and Language. After this, we had Culture and Context, where the remaining teams presented their presentation about their ideal nations. And we were done with our classes. We went back and chilled first and then did any pending work.

02nd April 2024

We first had our FAS meeting with our mentors. After that, we had Sustainability, Responsibility, and Managerial Ethics (SRME), where they were surprised to see how lethargic we looked. She was like, we need to bring up our energy, or how else will we survive? She taught us metrics to measure the Triple Bottom line and then asked us to read upon ITC's Triple Bottom Line performance to understand better. After this, the week's financial accounting party began. We had two continuous accounts sessions with 15-minute breaks between the two sessions. Sir gave us problems to solve on Inventory costing, and with a little bit of Bishakha's help, I finished the problems or worksheet in the class only. After, we went back to our hostel. It was also UTSAV day 02, and I went and watched their performance of folk dance. It was very vibrant, and we were executed, but it was so loud that I almost lost my hearing. It was alright but not very significant either. It was alright. After this, as we were heading back to our hostel, we bumped into Prof Vidya and Prof Muneza. After talking to them for a little while, we left to go to our hostel.

03rd April 2024

Today is Design Thinking Day, three continuous sessions; sir started the day by telling us how design thinking has multiple intricate steps beginning with the person or entity that we want to solve for, then observing them, taking interviews, doing secondary research, and trying to figure out what is the problem that we can solve for. What we solve for becomes design thinking. We presented our observations on the pani puri wala and tea point. After hearing both of the observations, I suggested that we take Tea Point and another business in the same category and observe them both. We, as a team, decided to take Tea Point and Chai Cafe. After this incident, we were back at the hostel, and we decided who would go for observations on which days and split our work. Today, I signed up for a gym membership for 1 month, and we went to work for the first time. It was not too much and just fine; after this, Mithra and I went straight to UTSAV with Sneha, Bishakha, and Harshitaa. We were later than yesterday, so there were only a few performances we could watch. It was really entertaining and fun to watch. After this, I ate from WGSHA's food truck, and it was good. We met Prof Vishnu and his wife, greeted them, and then clicked pretty photos of ourselves. And then I was finally done for the day.

04th April 2024

Today, we had class from 11:45 AM, so I woke up around 9:45 AM, showered, got ready, and went to Butterfly Cafe with Mithra to have our breakfast. Then, we boarded the bus and left for the campus. The first session was Sustainability, Responsibility, and Managerial Ethics (SRME), and today, the professor made us do an activity to figure out how companies measure their triple bottom line, research that, and forward it to her. We got the chemical industry, and we researched and found things that we believed should be metrics to measure tbl for the chemical industry. Harshitaa made the analysis on Canva and forwarded it to me, and I mailed it to Prof. After this, we had two continuous sessions of Financial Accounting, and sir made us solve problems on Allowance methods and bank reconciliation statements. After this, he also gave us the liabilities worksheet, which we need to bring to tomorrow's class. And finally, the day was over, and we went back to the hostel. Around 8 PM, Mithra and I went to Koin Circle to do our parts of the observation. Gauranshi and Mithra observed Chai Cafe while I observed Hyderabadi Tea Point. After 45 minutes, we again met each other. Gauranshi left after buying some necessities, and Mithra and I left for UTSAV today; it was amazing and worth watching. The performances were also so cool. It was the most fun today; even Sneha and Bishakha came by after a while.

05th April 2024

Today, we have four sessions; the first one is Culture and Context, where sir taught us Samakhya - Yoga and explained its different terms. Sir also told us that we need to present any topic on our own and let sir know beforehand. We, as a team, decided to present in the upcoming class on Ethics in the Indian Context. After this, we had SRME, and Ma'am gave us a case; it took us a long time to discuss, so in the next class, we will discuss our answers. Now, it was two Accounts sessions, and we solved liabilities and continued to practice more problems from the book. After this, once we came back, I went to the gym. She made me do some hard-core exercises. I was almost dead after today's session at Gymgym. It was an exhausting day, and I am so tired.

06th April 2024

After four sessions today and the last session of Scientific Thinking, we gave our insights as to what we learned over the course and what are our takeaways. After this, we filled out interim feedback forms for both our

Professors; the next class was Foundations of Psychology, and sir wasn't pleased with most of the class sitting at the end of the world and asked them questions about what he taught last class, if they could answer they were permitted to sit behind otherwise they had to come front and sit. As a frontbencher, I had tons of fun watching this. After this, we started with the session on Intelligence. The next two sessions were Financial Accounting, and we started the last worksheets and practiced and asked doubts that we had related to any topics or just the specific worksheet. After this, once we were back, Mithra and I went to the gym and worked out hard.

07th April 2024

It was Sunday, and it was my usual timetable. I also finished my part for our final Culture and Context presentation; I made some mess up while allotting work, which caused a lot of confusion. I fixed it and apologized as well, but it was chaotic. After this, I made sure all my other work was completed and that I had everything completed. After watching a few dramas here, I went to sleep.

08th April 2024

First, it taught us more about Samkyha and the many different thought processes behind it, and then we gave our presentation, which went well, and it was our last presentation as a team. We were a special team from Anthropology to Culture and Context. I think we won't have any more Sociology courses next semester, and it was really fun working with this unique team. After this was SRME, it was way too long to write it every single time.

First, we finished the case study, and then they asked if we liked this and wanted to do this next class as well, and we agreed. After this, we went back and divided the work for observations for the Design thinking project. No one had time for morning observation, so I took it up. I didn't go to the gym; instead, I took a nap and studied for Accounts, as tomorrow is the mid-semester paper for it. Wish me luck, guys, not only for the paper but also cause I have to get up extra early for the observation.

09th April 2024

I woke up at 6:45 AM and went to Koin Circle by 7 AM; there were few shops open. I had to be Tea Point's first customer; otherwise, it would be weird. I observed for roughly 40 minutes. Luckily, luckily, few customers came by, and I just had rose milk. Chai cafe, our other business, was closed, so I went back and had an early breakfast in the canteen. Then, I came back to my room, showered, and got ready. First, we had our exam, and it was alright; I would expect it to be better. After this, we had Psychology, where we finished Intelligence, and we informed sir that we would be conducting our experiment today. We quickly had our lunch and then began assembling our batch mates for the experiment. There were a few unforeseeable problems, and we apologized for those mistakes and quickly conducted our experiment. We also informed prof that we were done and told him that we had a few issues, and he said he would take care of them. After this, we had the SRME prof first teach us what a circular economy is and then start a discussion on the case study, which clearly was taking time, so she told us that we would continue this next class. After this was Culture and Context, and I was way too exhausted to listen to the class, so I honestly don't know what sir taught cause, at some point, I almost dozed off. After this, we went back to the gym. Boy, we did upper body, and my bicep muscles were sore. Me and I decided to go to a movie tomorrow; it is a language neither of us knows, so no one is at an advantage, and we are purely clueless.

10th April 2024

It was Design Thinking Day; our chance came almost near lunch break, so almost the entire lunch break went in telling sir our observations and how we needed to advance further; we even ate with sir and then finally started to divide our work based on what sir said to us. We also did some research on topics to be presented in microeconomics and mathematics. Then, we had SRME after three design thinking classes. Ma'am first made us conclude the case study and then started Business Canvas; however, a few kids in our class were being unruly, and that made her upset prof despite her continuous warnings, they did not stop. In the end, she left and told us. To learn on our own. Well, it ended pretty badly; after this, we left for the hostel. I ate some food in Butterfly and went to the movie. It was chaotic and funny. We lost our minds cause the storyline is weird and frustrating, and there were too many plot twists, like way too many. Anyway, we had tons of fun watching the movie. After this, we came back and chatted for a good while, as tomorrow was a holiday on account of Ramzan.

11th April 2024

That was supposed to be calm and nice, but it did not last long as my menstrual cycle decided to start today, and

I was dying in pain. I also informed my friends that my mood might swing very easily and that they shouldn't poke around me too much. I came back and decided to rest while giving myself a hot pack treatment; later in the evening, Mithra suggested going out for dinner to make my mood better. We laughed at Buddha, and the food was pretty tasty and nice. It did make my day a little better. Her being there always makes my day better. I heart you, Mithra baby girl.

12th April 2024

Now is the beginning of another weekend of Microeconomics; we had two sessions where sir started perfect competition and a little bit of monopoly. After this, we had financial accounting, where sir started stockholder's equity and explained a few basic terms and concepts. Lastly, we had SRME, where today we did Business Canvas for companies like Britania and Amul. We also learned the Sustainability Business Canvas and got our next assignment allotted to us, where we needed to work with our previous groups and do a Business Canvas and Sustainability Business Canvas with them. She also said that she would provide more about this soon. After this, we returned back, and I was tired either way as I also had my cramps killing me, but somehow, I pulled through the day.

13th April 2024

We had three economics classes, and sir continued to teach us monopoly and make us solve sums to figure it out better and make sense of it. He also informed us that his next visit will have a quiz, most probably, and presentations as well. He left us early, and we went back to our hostels and rested. After this, Mithra, Bishakha, and Harshitaa went to City Arena and played car racing for a good while. They had loads of fun. Bishakha is really good at this, and Mithra also plays well; as for Harshitaa, she was doing well until she suddenly wasn't. It was funny. Well, it clearly wasn't my forte, but I improved from last place I came to third. It was alright, as at least I learned how to reverse, which Harhistaa could clearly only do for a short while. Okay, jokes apart, we had loads of fun and then went to Planet Cafe to have our dinner; I had to eat vegetarian as tomorrow is our New Year, and Mom asked me to do so. I am not religious, but once in a blue moon, I listen to my parent's religious requests. After this, we were back, and I went to bed early as we also had class tomorrow, although it was Sunday. Oh, a unique thing that I found out about Varalika, other than her getting scared easily, is that she stitches really well; she stitched my pants and did a fantastic job. You are amazing, Varaaaaa.

14th April 2024

Today is Sunday, but I had to wake up early for class, get ready, and leave for breakfast. It was a rare Sunday breakfast, which I don't normally do, and then we had two classes on microeconomics where sir taught us game theory. It was very fun to learn, and it was a unique topic that excited me to listen to the class. Our quiz was on Friday, and our presentations will be on Saturday and Sunday. After this, we came back and had our lunch, and then I rested for a while. Then, I woke up and made a few diary entries. I clearly don't do it on the same day but rather on the weekend, forcing my memory to remember events. Mithra and I went to Chai cafe to interview them and their customers, and the interview went very well. We ate at All About Eggs and at Jo Momo's. Lately, places where I am eating have not accepted card payments, which is emptying my Google Pay wallet. Gosh, could you give me the power to get through this? I also had a jump scare, thinking tomorrow is our SRME quiz, but it turns out it is the day after. It stays the same as we now have two quizzes the day after, and I still need to prepare something. Please give me the strength to get through this, and someone helps Future Priyasha cause current Priyasha is being lazy.

CHAPTER ELEVEN

Explorations in Thought and Action

15th April 2024

Today, we had only two classes; the first one was Foundations of Psychology, where sir completed a tiny part of Intelligence, which he still needed to cover in the previous session, and then completed Language and wished us all the best for our quiz tomorrow. We at FAS B also went ahead and scheduled a virtual meeting for our psychology project at around 6 PM today. Next, we had culture and Context, where sir started Ayurveda and elaborated more on Yoga as well. Then we were done with our classes, returned to the hostel, and had lunch in our hostel's canteen. After this, I took a quick nap and then went to the gym with Mithra. We finished our workout quickly and headed back to the hostel, only to find out that the meeting had been postponed until an hour earlier. We instead went to Koin Circle and picked up the camera that we had given the owner of Chai Cafe. After this, I had to go to Tiger Circle, which was at the opposite end of Koin Circle, to get printouts of the log sheets, which was such a tiring job. I came back in time for the meeting, and sir taught us how to analyze the data that we received from our experiment.

After this, I showered and went out for dinner. I came back straight up after dinner; Hashitaa also narrated to us how, for the second time, a poor innocent puppy had licked scaredy cat Bishakha's leg, and the hell broke loose after that. I am telling you that Bishakha was a baby and needed to be protected at the time. After this, I did my laundry and sat down to revise the two quizzes. Maybe it could have been a better idea after all to put all that burden on future Priyasha yesterday, which is current Priyasha now.

16th April 2024

We had three classes today and two quizzes. The first session was Financial Accounting, where sir made us solve sums on stockholders' equity. It was challenging for Bishakha and me to understand, so we asked someone to teach it to us later. Now we had Culture and Context, and sir was explaining about Indian Aesthetics, but I wasn't paying full attention as I was preparing for SRME's quiz, which was during the first 20 minutes of our lunch break. The quiz was easy, and after this, we had our lunch. We started revising for the Psychology quiz, which was also right. Then we had our last session, which was Foundations of Psychology, and sir started Motivation and Emotion. After this, we came back to the hostel, and Mithra was working on sorting our data for analysis. We realized that one person needed to fill out our form, and one who hadn't participated in our experiment had filled out our form, causing confusion. I called up the kid who hadn't filled it, and he was sleeping; his roommate was in the library, and another of our teammates was also sleeping. As this was going nowhere, we decided to put a stop and get some rest. I clearly lost track of time as my body was sore from yesterday's workout and clearly missed my alarms as well. Mithra called me as she figured that I was still asleep. She fed me some food cause I was very hungry, and then we went down to discuss our Design Thinking project. After this, me and I went near Marena as she wanted ice cream and I wanted something to eat. I ordered food, and after it came, when I checked the time, it was 10:22 PM, and our curfew was in 8 minutes, and my good had just come. We got it packed and ran for our lives. We thought that we would not have to run anymore in the first semester as our curfew was moved up by an hour, but boy, we were wrong. It was such a chaotic and hectic way to end the day.

17th April 2024

it was Design Thinking Day, and we presented our design challenge to sir; we presented our idea to sir, and he told us to get our idea validated by the customers. After this, we had two sessions of Financial Accounting, which were the final classes. After this, the next two pending sessions were for assignment work. After this, once we went back, we went to the gym. On our way back to the gym, Mithra went to Koin Circle to validate our design idea, and it failed tremendously; no one wanted to order tea online, so they instead wanted to have it there only for the vibes and mood it sets. So we have to change plans.

18th April 2024

We had only one class today, and that was Culture and Context, and barely anyone came to class; sir asked two teams to present, and then I asked him a doubt that I had regarding the final report, and he clarified that. After this, once we returned back to the hostel, I did my laundry and then had my lunch. I took a nap and then started working on Economics; we have its final presentation this weekend. After this, I decided to go to the gym, and then once we got the gym back, we had dinner, and finally, the day was over.

19th April 2024

We have four sessions today, the first one being Foundations of Psychology; sir continued with emotions and completed it. After this, we had Culture and Context, where sir explained Indian aesthetics and its elements. After this, we had two continuous classes in Financial Accounting, where we started working on our final assignment, which was a very tiring and burdening assignment. There is so much analysis to do, and many ratios have yet to be taught to us, making the analysis process harder. Sir did tell me that he would be there any time to assist us; however, as everyone was struggling, he was super busy. After multiple changes in the hospitality industry, each one of us needed to work on a specific entity, so I was assigned to Ginger Hotels. I first started by downloading 5 years' worth of annual reports and then started working on the required ratios. Oh, ma dawgs! I am telling you this is so not easy and life draining. Why is all the work always distributed to us in the end? Man, never in my life have I undergone this kind of pressure. Uff, I want to rest.

20th April 2024

Today, we have three microeconomics classes, but I did not attend them as I was feeling under the weather because

I have not had any proper rest for the last two weeks. After having my breakfast, I and Mithra had an expert interview to take for our Design Thinking course. Thanks to Mithra and her father, we managed to get this interview with the CEO of Chai Kings, Mr Jahabar Sadique. He is a very humble, kind, and down-to-earth man; it was a great pleasure to interview him and learn so much from him. We finally had our design challenge from this discussion. After this, we started to work on the microeconomics presentation, which is tomorrow, Sunday, and our graded presentation. After this, we went to the gym for a change in gaming and a breather. Once again, we started working on the economics presentation.

21st April 2024

Today is the day of our presentations. It was a bumpy road, but somehow, we pulled through. We went over the time limit, and for me to present, my team and I had to beg sir for an extra minute, and then I rapped all the data out and left no crumbs. I should try rapping than this cause currently our schedule is so tight and suffocating. Once the presentations were over, we went back to the hostel and rested cause that's what I desperately needed. Tomorrow and the day after, we have a special workshop for our upcoming social internship, which is scheduled during our semester break.

22nd April to 05th May 2024

Update: I lost these entries and only realized this while editing.

CHAPTER TWELVE

Station Exam Stress has Arrived, Doors open to your left

06th May 2024

Today is the first paper of my end semester, and it opens with the banger called Microeconomics. It's not a difficult subject, but I seem to be terrible at getting knowledge on this one. I can understand a topic's intuition or solving angle, but I never understand both. So naturally, I was a little, no kidding, very much on the edge and tense during the preparations and the day of the exam as well. But I decided that I got this and walked into the exam hall. The iris scan, done before the paper opens for us in the E-pad (the weird tablet, which is very annoying), never works for me. So, as usual, I threw a tantrum like a baby girl, and then I had to call its father (the E-pad coordinator) to come and calm this kid down, and I started my paper. It went much better than last semester. Wow, I was surprised and happy that it was over, and I did not feel terrible like the previous one. So well done, PB!

After this, I came back to my room and started preparing for the next paper, which is (drum rolls) Sustainability, Responsibility, and Managerial Ethics. I rested a little first and then started prepping. This went well because it was a subject that was easy to relate and we had a great Professor (Prof. Purnima on the top!). Well, gotta catch up and get some sleep cause tomorrow Imma go slay the paper.

07th May 2024

I woke up feeling all prepped and great for the exam, but life really can be a Bad B sometimes, and it especially has to be one when it is crucial. Well, guess what? My iris scan gave up on me like any other day. A wife is pissed at her husband no matter what or nothing he does. But unlike all the times he gets her a rose, the delivery guy was late this time. Like the coordinator came to me exactly when the paper started, and I lost two precious minutes, but you might be like, still, you started writing the paper, so what worse could it get? Ironically, it was a lengthy paper in which more than half of the population struggled for the love of their life, but they could not finish it. But call it the woo of marriage; I somehow managed to finish in the last second. I wrote the last word, and the paper was submitted.

It was a battlefield, and we were all so tired after, but tomorrow I have Business Mathematics Paper, and I need practice. I do not know how, but I somehow pulled through after this war and studied until I felt like I would lose my mind and go to sleep.

08th May 2024

It is time for Mathematics! Okay, that was a bad one; the paper was good, considering how this has never been my favorite subject. The paper was over, and we returned back to our hostels. And it is my favorite subject tomorrow, Foundations of Psychology. I had a great time learning this subject, which means my revision time was also great; a few friends of mine had a few queries, so I did my best to explain those doubts, and hopefully, they will also do great. Unlike yesterday, today I went to bed on time and was peacefully resting.

09th May 2024

Guys, I am telling you this is my fave subject for a reason! It was my best paper so far, it felt so good completing it before time and walking out like a Gangster. Now, I was the last boss, Financial Accounting, another subject my brain needed to work on. Mahi and I were almost awake the entire night trying to figure out how not to fail! We did a barter system kind of revision where we learned different topics and then taught each other. Even at one point, we were chatting and laughing away all our funny moments as roommates, as there was a chance that she was planning to leave the course after this semester. But we realized we needed to sleep as tomorrow we needed to stay awake in the examination hall! Dear skies, please help her and me pass our paper tomorrow.

10th May 2024

It was my last paper today, Financial Accounting, and it was not as bad as I expected it to be; I finished the paper on time and was not feeling any kind of regret that I had initially thought I would. After the exam, Sneha, Mithrawr, and I went to Koin Home, a Korean restaurant in Coin Circle that has the greatest food known to mankind. The only red flag is the waiting time until the food is served. After this, once we were back, we got back to packing, and it was so chaotic because they told us that we had to vacate our rooms, which was one hell of a nightmare. We somehow sourced cardboard boxes as that was the best way to store and relocate all our things to the cloakroom or storage room. I was so exhausted from all the running around, and in the middle of that, Mithra forgot to give her key to the caretaker before leaving, so I asked her to leave it somewhere in Tiger Circle, and later, I picked it up. My father also arrived in Manipal and will be taking me back tomorrow. He was laughing at my situation, but he reminded me that this would be one hell of a core memory I will be laughing at in the future.

11th May 2024

I left early in the morning, around 8:30 AM, and told my goodbye to Mahi as she would be leaving and that she was a great roommate. Also, special thanks to Prof Krishna Prasad and Mrs. Parimala Hegde for helping us yesterday during the eviction process. Well, I will not bore you with my travel diaries because all I did was yap and gossip about life to my dad. We reached home, and I plan on enjoying my vacation until my social internship starts.

CHAPTER THIRTEEN

Team CARE forever

12th May to 19th May 2024

Nothing other than relaxing, eating good food, and meeting people happened here. But one honourable mention would be that Mithra The Mass, a.k.a MTM, turned 19 on 17th May 2024.

20th May to 24th May

First Week of Internship: I started my internship by finding my way from home to CARE (Charlie's Animal Rescue CentrE). I took Ola for the first day and then traveled by bus most days, other than a few days when it rained or was too late. Every day, I was required to work for 5 hours, starting from 11 AM to 4 PM, and this also included my 30-minute lunch break, which I was free to take any time. I had to get accustomed to all their different activities and gel with interns to make my life easier. I was interning with students from FLAME who were there a week earlier, and I had the pookiest and coolest manager. Anil was super easy to work around. I also got my CARE intern shirt this week. And it was really fun working with animals so I was having a great time!

27th May to 31st May 2024

An experienced Rookie: I had yet to start working full-time on my project of Improving the Barnyard, but I was doing a little bit here and there. Starting from setting up Guinea Pig's playground, which was fun and tiring because these tiny babies kept running away, and catching them was one hell of a work but really nice at the same time. I had also become a pro at shredding meat from boiled chicken, which was crucial as all the dogs and cats respected and loved me more when I did this task! I even had the honor of brushing the bunnies, who were all high and mighty. However, the highnesses gave me a few scratches here and there. Still, more or less, I had come to terms with their violent love language, but the days I brushed them, my rabbits at home did not resonate with me and often gave me the cold shoulder.

04th June to 07th June 2024

A pro Intern: Now let me take you through a few activities that I was an ace at! We had several CSR activities occurring every week; companies like JP Morgan, Goldman Sachs, Google, Delta Air, and many more came by for their CSR requirements. Those were the best days for us interns as we had a great time supervising and doing nothing unless we were supervising the god bathing team. Then, you were in for a ride. I also became better at taking visitors on tours alone. I even broke a record of a solid 2 hours of touring that even all the managers were surprised to hear about!

10th June to 14th June 2024

Baby Project Manager: By week four, I started to work more intensively on my project work. I had also spoken to my mentor for this internship, and it was none other than amazing Prof Muneza; she was my Business and Management Principles Professor from semester one. She was also pleased with my work and the updates provided to her so far, and she asked me not to stress about the job too much as I was doing well, and she would always be there to help and guide me if any problem arose. Moving back to my project, CARE had asked me to work in the Barnyard section and to try to improve awareness about barn animals like pigs, guinea pigs, and rabbits, who are often mistreated or not given the necessary attention and too many muddled opinions about them are present. After a discussion with my manager, we decided that we should first start with digital info plaques that can be uploaded to the website and physical copies to be displayed during touring.

17th June to 20th June 2024

Project Completion: With secondary research and field insights, I finally figured out how to create the plaques. It took some time, but eventually, I got a hang of it and completed it this week. The CSR activities were also getting more and more entertaining with every passing day; it was fun making cat houses out of cardboard boxes, bathing the puppies, and taking visitors on tour. It no longer felt like work and was more like a part of daily life. With only one week remaining, I wondered how I would be able to bid goodbye to this place, how much the animals were going to be on my mind, and how I would miss playing with them. But the tears are for the last day. For now, let's enjoy this beautiful journey.

24th June to 28th June 2024

Last week and Guru Intern: This journey is also ending, but I had no time to cry or throw a fit as now I was the senior intern in charge of teaching the new rookies the way around here before I left. It is as though the animals also knew I would be leaving because they grew fonder and more attached to me during this week. The adoption pups or naughty devils who always slipped away when I moved into their kennel were now much more well-behaved, or I got better at the job (either way, it is beneficial for me only). The rabbits no longer fought me like it was a war but instead would hop around me whenever I entered inside; the guinea pigs got a little bit more comfortable, but that one rooster in the barn never did. That boy was bloodthirsty. He always kicked me whenever I was inside, the only one I would surely not miss!

Special mention was given to all the managers, who were more like my buddies than supervisors, making work fun daily. Ms. Sudha, who was an inspirational leader, all the intern friends I worked with, my animal babies, and most importantly, myself for being such an amazing and iconic intern!